This book belongs to

_____

_____

_____

tiger tales
an imprint of ME Media, LLC
202 Old Ridgefield Road, Wilton, CT 06897
Published in the United States 2004
Originally published as Willem vliegt in Belgium 2003
By Uitgeverij Clavis, Amersterdam–Hasselt
Copyright © Uitgeverij Clavis, Amersterdam–Hasselt
CIP data is available
ISBN 1-58925-384-1
Printed in China
1 3 5 7 9 10 8 6 4 2

WHEN PIGS FLY!

by Stefan Boonen
Illustrated by Loufane

tiger tales

"Can pigs fly?" William asked his parents.
"Of course not," his dad grunted.
"Don't be silly," snorted his mom.
"I'm bored," William grumbled.
"Well then go and play," said his mom.
"Why don't you have a snack?" his dad suggested.

William shook his head. He didn't want
to roll in the mud, or eat bruised apples.
William didn't feel like doing anything.

"Let's play cowboys and Indians!" his brother
Tommy suggested.

"Cowboys are stupid." William said.

William ran out to the meadow where he
hid under the big apple tree. He just felt like
being alone.

"You look sad, William. Is something wrong?" asked Allie.

"Is flying very hard?" William asked quietly.

"Not for a goose!" she replied. Allie stretched her wings and off she flew.

"Wow!" William whispered. "I wish I could do that!"

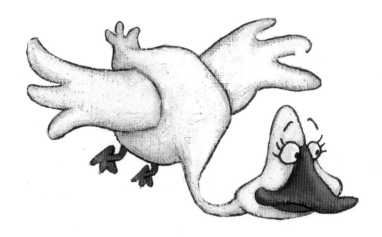

"If I flap with my legs, I could fly!"
he said to himself. "It can't be that hard!"
   William huffed and puffed as he
climbed the tree. Finally, he reached
the highest branch. "Phew!" he panted.
"I need a little rest!"
   "William! What are you doing?"
Tommy shouted up at him.

"Shhh!" William hissed. "Not so loud!"

But it was too late. Everybody was looking up at the big apple tree.

"What are you doing?" his dad shouted up at him.

William had jumped off the branch and
was flapping his legs wildly.
    "I'm flying!" he tried to yell to everyone.

SPLAT!

William crashed to the ground, right into a big mud puddle.

"Ow!" he cried.

"You're silly!" Tommy giggled. "Do you think you're a bird?"

Soon everyone was laughing at William, even the chickens!

All the laughing hurt William's feelings and his
bottom was bruised from his fall. Blushing deep red,
he ran back to his hiding place under the big apple tree.

"I almost flew!" he sobbed.

He looked up jealously at Allie, who was sitting on
the roof. "Wait a minute!" he said, as an idea popped
into his head. "Of course..."

William waited until the animals were taking their afternoon naps. The pigs were snoring in the mud, and the chickens were cozy on tufts of grass. Even Allie was asleep. While everyone was sleeping William quietly crept through the meadow.

By the pond he found three chicken feathers
and four dove feathers. Behind the big oak tree
he found some of Allie's old feathers. All through
the meadow he found more and more feathers.
Big ones, small ones, white ones, dark ones, thick
ones, and thin ones. With each feather he found
he let out a little grunt of joy.

"This is the best idea I've ever had!" William said. He took a deep breath and flopped into a mud puddle. He rolled and squirmed until he was completely covered with mud. He even dunked his head in to make sure his ears were covered.

William stuck his feathers into the wet mud that covered him. He put feathers on his belly, on his back, on his legs, on his sides, and even on his snout! He put a long chicken feather on his tail and two of Allie's feathers on his ears.

"I'm just like a bird now!" William thought happily. As fast as his little legs could carry him, he climbed back up to the highest branch of the big apple tree.

Just then, Tommy woke up from his nap and looked up at the tree. "There's a **monster** in the tree!" he cried.

"Shh!" William said, but it was too late.

Tommy's cries woke up all the animals, and everyone looked up at the tree.

"What is that?" they asked each other.

"We've never seen anything like it!" everybody said.

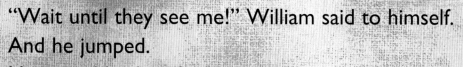

"Wait until they see me!" William said to himself. And he jumped.

He waved his legs faster and faster, feeling the wind through his feathers.

"I'm really flying!" William thought. He fluttered toward the roof.

"What's going on?" Allie cried.

William landed on the roof, grinning happily.

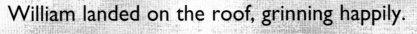

OOPS!   BANG!

He began to tumble down the roof. The hard
landing made the mud slide off William, taking the
feathers with it.
"It's William!" yelled Tommy. "He flew!"
The other pigs clapped and cheered.
"Wow!" the chickens clucked to each other.

Safely on the ground, William decided
flying was very hard work. He was very proud
of himself.

"See, Allie? Pigs can fly!" William called out.
"Well, at least one pig can!" she laughed.

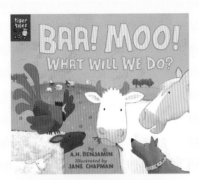

Baa! Moo! What Will We Do?
by A.H. Benjamin
illustrated by Jane Chapman
ISBN 1-58925-381-7

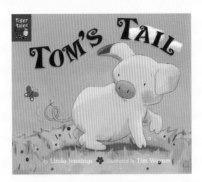

Tom's Tail
by Linda Jennings
illustrated by Tim Warnes
ISBN 1-58925-383-3

Snarlyhissopus
by Alan MacDonald
illustrated by Louise Voce
ISBN 1-58925-370-1

Explore the world of tiger tales!

More fun-filled and exciting stories await you!
Look for these titles and more at your local library or bookstore.
And have fun reading!

tiger tales

202 Old Ridgefield Road, Wilton, CT 06897

Through the Heart of the Jungle
by Jonathan Emmett
illustrated by Elena Gomez
ISBN 1-58925-380-9

The Very Lazy Ladybug
by Isobel Finn
illustrated by Jack Tickle
ISBN 1-58925-379-5

Love Is a Handful of Honey
by Giles Andreae
illustrated by Vanessa Cabban
ISBN 1-58925-353-1